The Bronze Dog

This book is edited and designed by the Editorial Committee of *Cultural China* series

Story and Illustrations: Li Jian
Translation: Yijin Wert

Copy Editor: Anna Nguyen
Editor: Wu Yuezhou
Editorial Director: Zhang Yicong

Senior Consultants: Sun Yong, Wu Ying, Yang Xinci
Managing Director and Publisher: Wang Youbu

ISBN: 978-1-60220-998-5

Address any comments about *The Bronze Dog* to:

Better Link Press
99 Park Ave
New York, NY 10016
USA

or

Shanghai Press and Publishing Development Co., Ltd.
F 7 Donghu Road, Shanghai, China (200031)
Email: comments_betterlinkpress@hotmail.com

Printed in China by Shenzhen Donnelley Printing Co., Ltd.

3   5   7   9   10   8   6   4   2

青铜狗
The Bronze Dog

A Story in English and Chinese

By Li Jian

Translated by Yijin Wert

Better Link Press

In a mountain village of southern China, there were two brothers who lived a very poor life together.

在中国南方的山村里，生活着一对兄弟，他们相依为命，过着贫苦的生活。

One day, the elder brother wanted to dig out a vegetable garden in their backyard. After he dug a hole deep to his waist, his hoe suddenly hit something hard with a big noise.

　　有一天，哥哥想在院子里挖一口菜窖。当他挖到齐腰深的时
候，突然听到铛啷一声响，他的锄头碰到了硬东西……

He saw, under the dirt, a bronze dog with beautiful and fine carvings on his body.

泥土里露出一只青铜狗，身上的花纹非常精美。

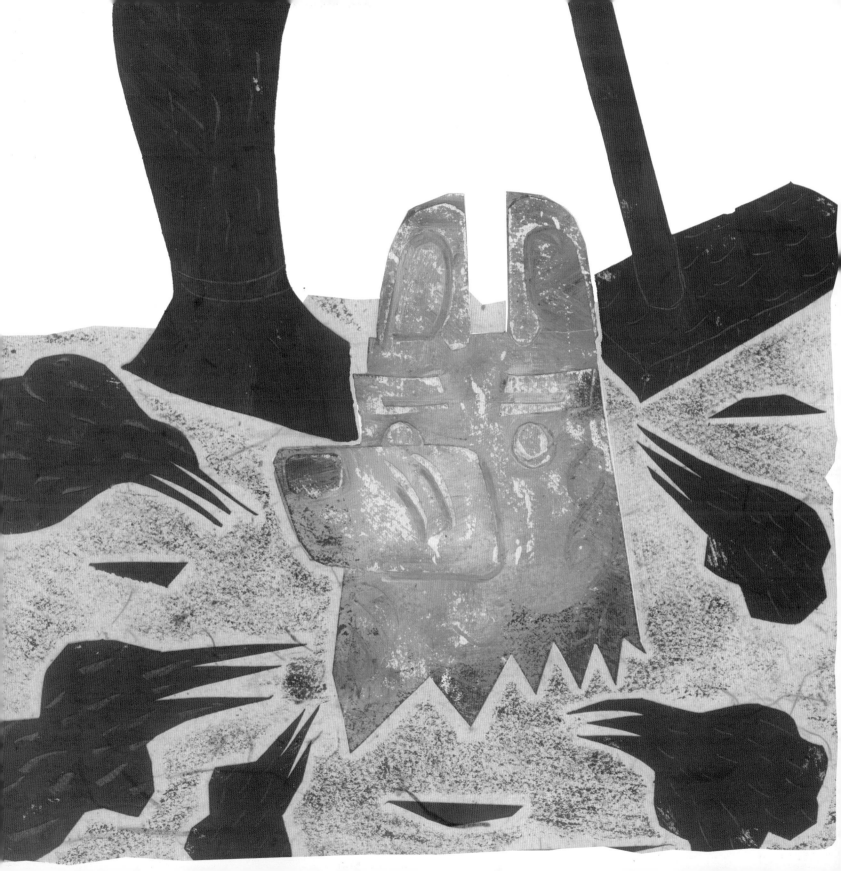

He called his younger brother over immediately, who looked
very surprised and excited as he saw the dog. He knew anything
made of bronze could be sold for a high price in the city.

哥哥忙叫弟弟来看。弟弟又惊又喜，他曾听人说，青铜的物品在京城能换很多钱。

The two brothers started to plan on how to spend the money after selling the bronze dog.

"We could build a house with three rooms!"

"We could buy all the good foods we want!"

"Yes, we could make several sets of new outfits!"

"Also, we could buy two strong oxen to plow the fields for us!"

哥俩开始盘算着卖了青铜狗以后，该怎么花这笔钱。
"我们要盖三间新房！"
"要买很多好吃的东西！"
"对对对，还要做几身新衣服！"
"还要买两头壮实的牛，帮咱们犁地！"

Just at that moment, they noticed that the bronze dog had grown huge. He wiggled his tail, opened his big mouth and picked up the elder brother.

正说着，这只青铜狗突然变得很大，甩着尾巴，张开大嘴，一口咬住哥哥。

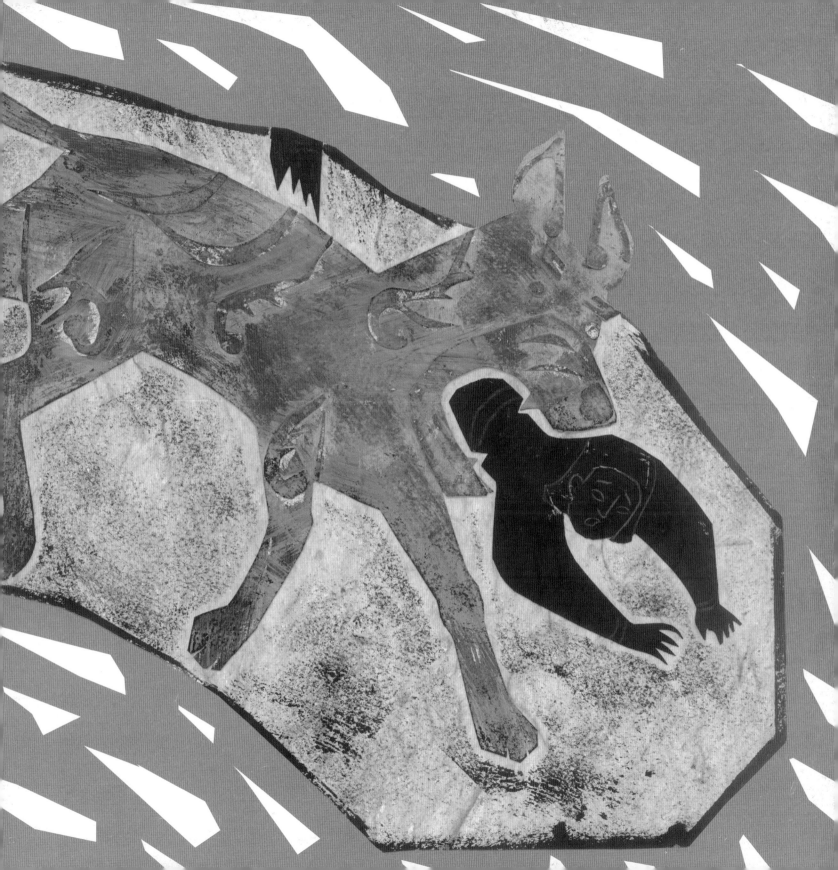

The bronze dog engulfed the elder brother completely.
The only thing left was his hat.

The younger brother grabbed the oil lamp on the table
and hit the head of the dog with it.

青铜狗吞下哥哥，只剩他的帽子丢在一边。
弟弟一把抓起桌子上的油灯砸在青铜狗的头上。

The younger brother then tied the dog's neck with a rope before he realized what had happened.

The younger brother was anxious to save his brother. He found a hammer and was about to hit the dog's head. Just at that moment, the bronze dog opened his mouth and said, "I beg you not to hit my head."

趁青铜狗一愣神的功夫，弟弟用绳子拴住了它的脖子。

弟弟急着救哥哥，找来锤子，准备砸向青铜狗的头。这时，青铜狗却开口说话了："求你不要砸我的头。"

The bronze dog then blew out some smoke around their house. The slum house suddenly turned out to be a beautiful house with three rooms. "If you don't hit my head, this new house is yours," said the bronze dog.

青铜狗朝破茅屋吐出一圈烟雾。茅屋瞬间变成了三间漂亮的新房子。"只要不砸我的头，这三间新房子就送给你了！"青铜狗说。

"No, we could still live in the old house if we don't have the new one, but I would be very lonely without my brother. Please return my brother to me now!"

"我才不换呢！没有新房子，可以住在破茅屋里。可是没有哥哥，我会很孤单，快把哥哥还给我！"

Once again, the bronze dog blew out some smoke around the table. Suddenly the table was covered with variety of delicious foods and beautiful clothes. "If you don't hit my head, all these foods and clothes are yours," said the bronze dog.

青铜狗又往桌子吐出一圈烟雾，桌子上一下子摆满了各种糕点和精美的衣服，"只要不砸我的头，这些糕点和新衣服，都送给你了！"青铜狗说。

"No, we could still live very happily without these foods and beautiful clothes, but I would be very lonely without my brother. Please return my brother to me now!"

"我才不换呢！没有糕点，没有漂亮的衣服，我们照样可以过得很开心，可是没有哥哥，我会很孤单，快把哥哥还给我！"

Once again, the bronze dog blew out some smoke in the yard. Suddenly two strong oxen stood in the yard. "If you don't hit my head, these two oxen are yours," said the bronze dog.

青铜狗又朝院子里吐出一圈烟雾，两头壮实的耕牛突然冒出来，"只要不砸我的头，这两头牛就送给你了！"青铜狗说。

"No, without the help from the oxen, we still were able to plow the field even though it is hard labor, but I would be very lonely without my brother! Please return my brother to me now!"

"我才不换呢！没有耕牛，我们累一点，依然可以把地耕种好，可是没有哥哥，我会很孤单，快把哥哥还给我！"

The bronze dog nodded his head and said, "You two are inseparable brothers. I dare not tear you apart." Then he opened his mouth.

青铜狗点头说道："你们是好兄弟，我怎么忍心分开你们呢？"说罢，它张开嘴。

When the younger brother saw his brother's hand in the mouth of the bronze dog, he grabbed his hand immediately and pulled him out of the dog's mouth with all his strength.

　　哥哥的一只手从青铜狗的嘴里伸出来，弟弟连忙抓住，
用力把哥哥拉了出来。

Then the bronze dog started to shake his body. Pieces of bronze were gradually falling off his body. In the blink of an eye, the bronze dog turned into a real dog.

青铜狗突然抖动身体，青铜碎片纷纷落下，眨眼间，青铜狗变成了一只真正的狗。

Seeing the two brothers holding each other and crying, the dog said, "I have been searching for kind masters for a long time. I believe that I have found them today."

看着抱头痛哭的兄弟俩，狗说道："我一直在寻找善良的主人，今天终于找到了你们这一对好兄弟。"

The dog gave the house, the foods, the clothes and the oxen to the brothers. He lived with them happily ever after.

狗把房子、糕点、衣服和耕牛都送给了两兄弟，从此和他们幸福地生活在一起。

The Loyal Dog

The Dog occupies the eleventh position in the Chinese zodiac. It is straight forward, honest, loyal and dependable. It gets along very well with others, but sometimes can be very stubborn.

忠诚的狗

狗在十二生肖中排第十一，纯朴正直，忠实可靠，能与其他人和睦相处。但有时也非常固执。

Lunar Years of the Dog in the Western Calendar

4 February 1922 to 4 February 1923   4 February 1934 to 4 February 1935

4 February 1946 to 3 February 1947   4 February 1958 to 3 February 1959

4 February 1970 to 3 February 1971   4 February 1982 to 3 February 1983

4 February 1994 to 3 February 1995   4 February 2006 to 3 February 2007

4 February 2018 to 3 February 2019   4 February 2030 to 3 February 2031

4 February 2042 to 3 February 2043

Cultural Explanation

Stone relief is a form of sculpture that was popular in the Han Dynasty (206 BC –AD 220). The stone reliefs were put in ancestral halls and tombs as architectural decorations by local artists. Some stone relief pictures depict rich daily life, while the others depict figures from fantasy fairy tales. This picture book adopts the stone relief carving style from the Chinese Han Dynasty.

画像石是中国汉代（前206–220）民间艺人雕刻在祠堂、墓室等的石刻装饰画，有丰富的日常生活，也有奇幻的神仙故事。本书绘画即是汉代画像石的风格。